for inari

LOTHIAN
Children's Books

A Lothian Children's Book

Published in Australia and New Zealand
by Hachette Australia Pty Limited
Level 17, 207 Kent Street, Sydney
NSW 2000
www.hachettechildrens.com.au

Copyright © Shaun Tan 2001

First published 2001
Reprinted 2001, 2002, 2004, 2007, 2008, 2010
Paperback edition published 2002

National Library of Australia
Cataloguing-in-Publication data:

Tan, Shaun.
The red tree.
ISBN 978 0 7344 1087 0
I. Title.
A823.3

Design by Shaun Tan
Colour reproduction by Scott Digital,
Port Melbourne
Printed in China by
Everbest Printing Co Ltd

sometimes the day begins
with nothing to look forward to

and things go from bad to worse

darkness

overcomes you

nobody understands

the world is a

deaf machine

sometimes you wait

and wait

and wait

and wait

and wait   and wait

and wait   but nothing ever happens

wonderful things

are

passing

you

by

terrible fates are
inevitable

sometimes
you just don't know
what you are
supposed to
do

or

who

you   meant
        are

                        to

                        be

or

where
you are

and the day seems to end
the way it began

but suddenly there it is
right in front of you

bright and vivid

quietly waiting

just as you imagined it would be